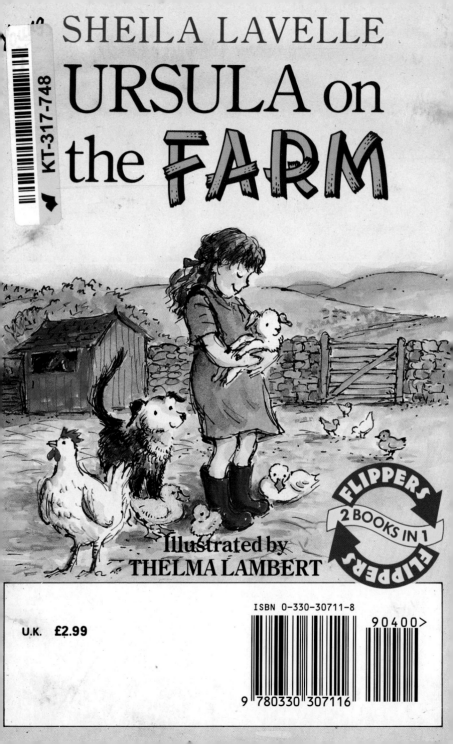

SHEILA LAVELLE

URSULA on the FARM

Illustrated by
THELMA LAMBERT

FLIPPERS
2 BOOKS IN 1
FLIPPERS

ISBN 0-330-30711-8

U.K. **£2.99**

90400>

9 780330 307116

URSULA AT THE ZOO and URSULA ON THE FARM

Ursula is an ordinary little girl, but she has a special secret. She can turn herself into a bear.

In *Ursula at the Zoo* Ursula changes into a bear and helps to cheer up a lonely old friend in the zoo.

In *Ursula on the Farm* Ursula and her friends visit Mr Ford's farm where they meet all kinds of animals and Ursula makes a daring rescue!

SHEILA LAVELLE

Ursula on the Farm

illustrated by Thelma Lambert

Young Piper

First published 1987 in The Cartwheels Series by
Hamish Hamilton Children's Books
This Young Piper edition first published 1988 by
Pan Books Ltd, Cavaye Place, London SW10 9PG
9 8 7 6
Text copyright © Sheila Lavelle 1987
Illustrations copyright © Thelma Lambert 1987
ISBN 0 330 30711 8
Printed and bound in Great Britain by
Cox & Wyman Ltd, Reading, Berkshire

Ursula had blue eyes and brown hair
and a dimple in her cheek when she
smiled. She looked just like an ordinary
little girl.

But Ursula had a very special secret.
Ursula could turn herself into a bear.

She had found the spell in a book in the library. All she needed was a currant bun, filled with a mixture of porridge oats and honey.

A few magic words, and hey presto! Ursula would turn into a real, live bear.

Ursula had lots of fun being a bear. And turning back into herself again afterwards was simple.

A plate of beefburgers and chips did the trick, every single time.

One day, when Ursula was at school,
Miss Plum came smiling into the
classroom with a letter in her hand.

"Listen, children," she said. "This is
from Mr Ford, the farmer. We've all
been invited to spend a day on his
farm."

There was a lot of noise while
everybody shouted "Hooray!" and
"Whoopee!"

Ursula was very excited. She had never been to a farm before.

"Will there be animals?" she asked the teacher.

"Yes, Ursula," smiled Miss Plum. "There'll be cows and pigs, sheep and goats, ducks and hens, and maybe even some baby lambs."

Ursula ran home to tell Aunt Prudence all about it.

Aunt Prudence didn't know Ursula's secret. But she did know that Ursula was very fond of currant buns.

So when she packed Ursula's lunch-bag on the day of the visit, she put in an extra-large one.

And she didn't forget Ursula's favourite filling of porridge oats and honey.

"Can I have a beefburger as well?" begged Ursula. "And a few chips?"

"Chips?" said Aunt Prudence in astonishment. "They'll get cold."

"I like cold chips," said Ursula. And she was very pleased when kind Aunt Prudence did as she asked. Now Ursula had everything she needed to turn into a bear and back again.

In the bus, everybody sang "Old
Macdonald had a farm". Even Miss
Plum joined in.

Ursula looked out of the window at the
trees and the green fields.

Mr Ford was waiting for them at the
farm gate, with a black and white
sheepdog called Ben.

The children climbed out of the bus
and gazed about them with round eyes.

Ben put his nose into Ursula's bag and
sniffed at the beefburger.

"That's not for you," laughed Ursula.

"Come along, everybody," said the
farmer. And he showed them all round
the farm.

They saw the cows being milked in the
sheds, and they fed the baby calves.

The boys helped the farmer's wife to
give the pigs their bucket of mash.

There were sixteen pink piglets in the
sty.

The girls fed the goats and gave some corn to the ducks and hens.

Ursula collected one hundred and twenty-seven eggs.

"What good workers you are!" said Mrs Ford. And she gave them all milk and biscuits in the farm kitchen.

"Now," said the farmer, "let me find you some more jobs."

"We haven't seen any lambs," said Ursula suddenly.

"The lambs aren't born yet," smiled the farmer. "The sheep are still out on the hill-side. I'm sending Ben to fetch them home today, so the lambs can be born in the warm barn."

"Let me go with him," begged Ursula.

"It's a long way," warned the farmer. "But Ben will make sure you don't get lost. You'd better take your lunch with you."

Ursula put her bag over her shoulder and set off up the hill, with Ben leading the way.

Ben was a very clever dog. He ran here and there, collecting the sheep together and turning them towards home.

But one sheep didn't want to come.

It stood on the edge of a rocky cliff, baa-ing loudly.

Ben ran behind the sheep to drive it
away from the edge. But the sheep
stamped its foot and would not move.

Ursula looked over the cliff.

"Oh, no!" she gasped.

A tiny lamb, only a few hours old,
had fallen into a deep gully. It was lying
on a ledge near the bottom, bleating in a
weak small voice.

Ben dashed backwards and forwards along the top of the gully and whined.

The sides were too steep, and there was no way he could get down to help the lamb.

Ursula knew she couldn't climb down either.

But she knew somebody who could.

In less than a minute, Ursula had
unpacked the magic currant bun and
was munching away so fast she almost
choked.

"I'M A BEAR, I'M A BEAR, I'M A
BEAR," she muttered. "I'M A BEAR,
I'M A BEAR, I'M A BEAR."

Ben gave a sudden yelp and his ears stood on end.

The girl in the blue dress had vanished.

And there, in her place, was a small brown bear.

With the lunch-bag on her shoulder,
Ursula Bear lowered herself over the
edge of the gully.

Down and down she went, hanging on
to rocks and brambles with her sharp
claws.

And at last she reached the ledge
where the little lamb was lying.

The lamb bleated in fright when it saw the bear.

"There, there," Ursula growled softly. "I won't hurt you."

And she gently lifted the baby lamb into the bag.

Ben raced about barking when he saw
Ursula scrambling back up the gully.

She reached the top at last, and soon
the lamb was safely by its mother's side.

Ursula sat down for a rest, and to eat
her beefburger.

"RAEB A M'I, RAEB A M'I, RAEB A
M'I," she growled, stuffing beefburger
and chips into her mouth with her paws.

Ben wagged his tail hopefully, and his
mouth watered as he watched every
single mouthful.

Ursula saved him the very last bite.

And in no time at all Ursula was
herself again, much to Ben's joy and
relief.

He rounded up the sheep and set off
down the hill towards the farm, his tail
waving like a flag.

Ursula followed with the lamb in her
arms.

Mr Ford was amazed when he saw the
lamb.

"It's lucky you were there to bring it
home," he said. "Come inside, Ursula.
Everybody's having a nice big tea."

"Ben's earned one, too," said Ursula.
And she shared her scones and jam
and cream with her new friend.

Also available in the Flippers series:

by Linda Allen
Illustrated by Margaret Chamberlain

MRS SIMKIN AND THE MAGIC WHEELBARROW

No one believes Mrs Simkin when she says that her new wheelbarrow is a magic one until they see the wonderful magic for themselves. Before long, everyone wants a wheelbarrow like Mrs Simkin's!

MRS SIMKIN AND THE VERY BIG MUSHROOM

One morning Mrs Simkin wakes up to find an enormous mushroom growing in her garden, but instead of cutting it down, she makes use of the mushroom in lots of clever – and hilarious – ways.

Now flip this book over and read
URSULA ON THE FARM

URSULA AT THE ZOO
Now flip this book over and read

Also available in the Flippers series:

HARRY'S AUNT and HARRY'S HORSE
by Sheila Lavelle
Illustrated by Jo Davies

Harry didn't know his aunt was a witch until she took off for a ride on her broomstick!
    And Harry was also surprised to find that his aunt could turn into any animal she felt like. The trouble was Harry never knew what animal she would change into next . . .

Both these entertaining stories about Harry and his unpredictable aunt are ideal for children who are just starting to read for themselves.

Flippers are a special part of the Young Piper list for readers aged between 5 and 8.

Each Flipper contains two complete books, printed back to back. When you've finished one, flip the book over and read the other!

Ursula at the Zoo and *Ursula on the Farm* are written specially for children in the early stages of beginning to read for themselves.

Sheila Lavelle was born in County Durham in 1939. As a child, she loved reading and wrote plays, stories and poetry. However, her plans to be a writer were put aside for a few years, during which time she married her husband, Derek, had two sons and later worked as a teacher.

Her first book came out in 1977, and since then she has never stopped writing for children, with several new books coming out each year. Her sons are now grown up and she lives in Bourne End, Buckinghamshire, with her husband, two dogs and two cats.

SHEILA LAVELLE

Ursula at the Zoo

illustrated by Thelma Lambert

Young Piper

First published 1986 in The Cartwheels Series by
Hamish Hamilton Children's Books
This Young Piper edition first published 1988 by
Pan Books Ltd, Cavaye Place, London SW10 9PG
9 8 7 6
Text copyright © Sheila Lavelle 1986
Illustrations copyright © Thelma Lambert 1986
ISBN 0 330 30711 8
Printed and bound in Great Britain by
Cox & Wyman Ltd, Reading, Berkshire

Ursula was a girl who loved bears.
Big bears and little bears, fat bears and
thin bears, furry bears and bare bears,
Ursula loved them all.

Ursula loved bears so much she wanted
to BE one.

Ursula lived with her Aunt Prudence.
"How can I turn into a bear?"
she asked Aunt Prudence one day.
"Silly," laughed Aunt Prudence.
"I like you just as you are."
But Ursula still wanted to be a bear.

In the library Ursula found a book of magic spells. On page one hundred and sixty-three it said, "How a little girl can turn into a bear."

Ursula's eyes grew round with delight.

Ursula copied down the spell and
hurried home.

In the kitchen she mixed together two
spoonfuls of porridge and one spoonful of
honey. She put the mixture into a currant
bun.

Down in the garden shed Ursula sat on
a pile of sacks.

"I'M A BEAR, I'M A BEAR, I'M A
BEAR," she said, over and over again.
And she ate every scrap of the magic bun.

Ursula looked at her reflection in the window of the house. She saw a furry face, two round ears and a pair of black twinkling eyes. She stared and stared.

"It's me!" she cried in a strange, growly voice. "I'm a bear!" And she turned cartwheels all over the lawn.

The spell had worked, and all she needed to turn back into herself again was a plate of beefburgers and chips. Now Ursula could turn herself into a bear whenever she liked.

Ursula had lots of fun turning into a bear, and she had many adventures.

One Friday afternoon she went to visit her favourite bear of all. He was a big brown bear called Mr Brown, and he lived in the zoo. Ursula often took him one of her special porridge-and-honey buns on her way home from school.

But today Mr Brown wouldn't eat his
bun. He sat in a corner of his cage with
his chin on his paws staring at the
ground. He looked very miserable.

"He hasn't eaten anything for days," the keeper told her, looking worried. "He's making himself ill. I don't know what to do."

Ursula pushed the bun through the bars, but Mr Brown turned his big head away and closed his eyes.

"I think he's feeling lonely,"
said Mr Monty. "He needs another
bear to keep him company. There's one
coming from Bristol in a few days time.
That ought to cheer him up." And off
he went to give the penguins their
bucket of fish.

Ursula stared at Mr Brown's sad face.
A few days time might be too late. Mr
Brown might even die.

There was only one thing to do, and
Ursula did it. She reached through the
bars and picked up Mr Brown's currant
bun.

Ursula hid behind the elephant-house
and gobbled the bun as fast as she could.

"I'M A BEAR, I'M A BEAR, I'M A
BEAR," she mumbled. The elephant
looked very surprised.

A few moments later the elephant was even more surprised. The little girl in the blue dress had suddenly disappeared. And in her place a small brown bear was dancing gleefully about in the grass.

The magic had worked, and Ursula was a bear once more.

People started to run about, shouting.
The monkeys screamed in their cages,
and the lions and tigers began to roar.

"Help! A bear has escaped!" cried a fat
lady in a purple dress. Mr Monty hurried
to see what was going on.

"Well I'm blowed! It's a bear!"
said Mr Monty, scratching his head.
"I don't know where you came from, but
I know where you're going." And he
picked Ursula up in his arms and
carried her to Mr Brown's cage.

The keeper opened the cage and pushed
Ursula inside.

Mr Brown lifted his head and stared.

"Hello, Mr Brown," growled Ursula.
"I've come to play with you." She put her
paws round the great bear's neck and
gave him a hug.

Mr Brown came to life at once. He
rolled over on his back and waved his
paws in the air. He scampered about like
a cub, chasing Ursula round and round
the cage. And he ate every scrap of the
dinner that Mr Monty pushed through the
bars.

Ursula had never had so much fun in her life. She showed Mr Brown how to stand on his head and turn cartwheels, and she rode round the cage on his back.

The hyena in the next cage laughed himself silly.

All too soon the afternoon was over and it was time for Ursula to say goodbye. Mr Brown seemed to understand when she told him another bear was on his way. He shook Ursula's paw.

Then Ursula lay down on the floor of the cage, clutching her stomach and groaning.

Mr Monty came running at once. He unlocked the cage and bent down to see what was wrong with the little bear. Ursula leapt up, dodged past the keeper's feet and was out of the cage in a flash.

She scrambled up a fence and down the other side, and found herself on the edge of the park. It was tea time, and not many people were about, so nobody noticed as she scampered thankfully away towards home.

Now Ursula had to turn into herself again, and only beefburger and chips would do the trick. She was very glad when she reached the High Street and found the Burger Bar still open.

The tables were all empty except for one in the corner where a boy in a leather jacket sat reading a newspaper.

Ursula's eyes shone when she saw that he had left most of his carton of beefburger and chips. She leapt up onto the table, grabbed the carton of food and raced out again.

The boy's mouth fell open in surprise, and the waitress dropped her tray.

Safely home at last, Ursula hid in the garden shed to eat her beefburger and chips. And while she ate them she muttered the magic words backwards.

"RAEB A M'I, RAEB A M'I, RAEB A M'I," she growled, licking tomato sauce from her paw.

In no time at all Ursula was quite herself again. She ran up the garden path and let herself in at the kitchen door.

She hoped Aunt Prudence hadn't made beefburger and chips for tea.